For Ry and Birdie.
Wishing you everything odd, extraordinary,
strange, and sensational!
—N.E.

For Skyler, with love
—L.E.

Dill & Bizzy: An Odd Duck and a Strange Bird
Text copyright © 2016 by Nora Ericson
Illustrations copyright © 2016 by Lisa Ericson
Library of Congress Cataloging-in-Publication Data
Ericson, Nora.
  Dill & Bizzy: an odd duck and a strange bird / by Nora Ericson ; illustrated by Lisa Ericson. — First edition.
    pages cm
  Summary: When Bizzy, an admittedly strange bird, meets Dill, a self-professed ordinary duck, it is the start of a most unusual friendship.
  ISBN 978-0-06-230452-0 (hardcover)
  [1. Eccentrics and eccentricities—Fiction. 2. Friendship—Fiction. 3. Ducks—Fiction. 4. Birds—Fiction. 5. Humorous stories.] I. Ericson, Lisa, illustrator. II. Title.
PZ7.E72577 Dil 2016   2013051291
[E]—dc23   CIP
                                                                                                                                       AC

The artist used ink on paper colored digitally to create the illustrations for this book.
Typography by Dana Fritts
15 16 17 18 19 SCP 10 9 8 7 6 5 4 3 2 1
❖
First Edition

Dill & Bizzy
An Odd Duck and a Strange Bird

By Nora Ericson   Illustrated by Lisa Ericson

HARPER
An Imprint of HarperCollinsPublishers

Dill was a duck. An ordinary duck.
At least that's what he thought.

Bizzy was a bird. A strange bird. She swooped in with a splash.

"I am a strange bird!" cried Bizzy.

"I can see that," said Dill.

"Are you an odd duck?" asked Bizzy.
"No!" said Dill. "I'm an ordinary duck!
Not odd at all."

"How sad," said Bizzy. "An odd duck and a strange bird could be friends."

"I am not an odd duck," said Dill. He didn't need to be friends with a strange bird. At least that's what he thought.

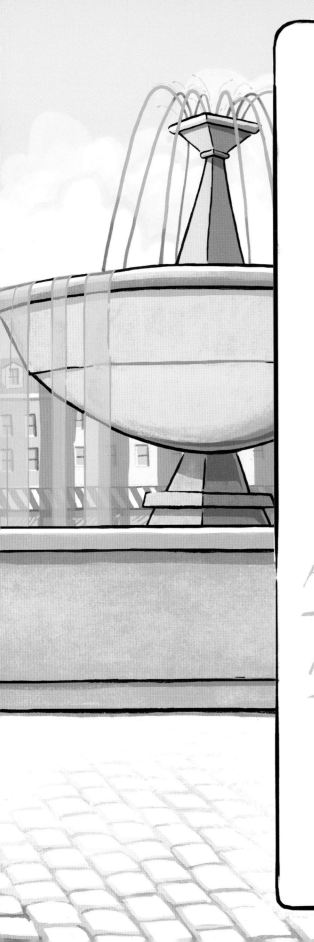

"I wish you were an odd duck," said Bizzy. "An odd duck would come along with me for a bicycle ride."

"I am not an odd duck," said Dill.

"But I'll take the unicycle!"

Bizzy shouted, "No wings!"
Dill shouted, "No wings,
no feet!"

"I wish you were an odd duck," said Bizzy. "An odd duck would have lunch with me at the pretzel stand."

"I am not an odd duck," said Dill.

"I always have lunch
with the hot dog man."

"What a fabulous fellow!" said Bizzy.
"He does seem to like you," said Dill.

Bizzy had a bun with all the fixings.
Dill had the same, with
extra pickles.

"I wish you were an odd duck," said Bizzy. "An odd duck would fly some loop-the-loops with me!"

"I am not an odd duck,"
said Dill.

"I just fly a little to the left."

Bizzy looped and Dill
swooped. Then Bizzy
swooped and Dill looped.

"I'm getting dizzy," said Dill. "And my fountain needs tidying."

"Oh, let me help you!" said Bizzy. "I make an excellent duster."

"That's better," said Dill. "Now all it needs is some color."

Dill and Bizzy admired their work. Not bad for a strange bird and an ordinary duck.

"Are you *sure* you aren't an odd duck?" asked Bizzy.

"Of course I'm sure!" said Dill. "I'm perfectly ordinary!"

yodelay hee-hoo

"An odd duck could yodel with me!" said Bizzy.

"You'll have to settle for my ordinary quack," said Dill.

QUACK!
QUACK!
QUACK!
QUACK! QUACK!
QUACK!
QUACK!
QUACK!
QUACK!
QUACK!
QUACK!
QUACK!

"An odd duck could join my strange bird boogie!"

"I'll just do my ordinary duck dance."

"Upside down!"

"Take a bow, ordinary duck!" said Bizzy.

"They must be cheering for you, strange bird," said Dill. "They think you're sensational!"

Now Bizzy was a strange, hot, and tired bird.
She swooped down with a splash.
  "I'm glad you don't have to be an odd duck to
take a dip with me," she said.

Now Dill was an ordinary, hot, and tired duck.
At least that's what he still thought.
"I'm afraid I cannot swim," he said. "Would
you like a floatie?"

Bizzy sighed. "How I wish you were an odd duck. An odd duck and a strange bird could be *the best* of friends."

Dill thought about the unicycle, his tasty lunch, and the loop-the-loops. He looked at his beautiful fountain.

"Maybe I could learn to be *a tiny bit* of an odd duck," said Dill, at last. "Because it might be nice to be best of friends with a strange bird. A strange and sensational bird like you."

"And I think I could try to be best of friends with an ordinary duck," said Bizzy. "A perfectly *extra*-ordinary duck like you."